Humphrey's
Creepy-Crawly
Camping Adventure

Betty G. Birney
illustrated by Priscilla Burris

PUFFIN BOOKS
An Imprint of Penguin Group (USA)

PUFFIN BOOKS
Published by the Penguin Group
Penguin Group (USA) LLC
375 Hudson Street, New York, NY 10014

USA | Canada | UK | Ireland | Australia
New Zealand | India | South Africa | China
penguin.com
A Penguin Random House Company

Published simultaneously in the United States of America by G. P. Putnam's
Sons and Puffin Books, imprints of Penguin Young Readers Group, 2015

THE LIBRARY OF CONGRESS HAS CATALOGED
THE G. P. PUTNAM'S SONS EDITION AS FOLLOWS:
Birney, Betty G.
Humphrey's creepy-crawly camping adventure / Betty G. Birney ;
illustrated by Priscilla Burris.
pages cm.—(Humphrey's tiny tales)
ISBN 978-0-399-17227-4 (hardcover)
Summary: "Humphrey goes on a backyard camping adventure with his
classmates and meets all kinds of outdoor creatures—even some scary
ones"—Provided by publisher.
[1. Camping—Fiction. 2. Hamsters—Fiction. 3. Fear—Fiction.] I. Burris,
Priscilla, illustrator. II. Title.
PZ7.B5229 Hq 2015
[Fic]—dc23
2014015695

Puffin Books ISBN 978-0-14-751459-2

Printed in the United States of America
Design by Ryan Thomann

3 5 7 9 10 8 6 4 2

A *snake?!*

I heard some shuffling and whispering kinds of sounds.

"Something's out there," Sayeh whispered.

"It sounds like it's near the tent," Miranda said. "Let's see."

The girls quietly picked up their flashlights and tiptoed to the tent flap.

"There's something in the grass," Gail whispered.

"It's a . . . great . . . big . . . snake!" Heidi shouted.

"Eeek!" the girls screamed.

They raced toward the house, leaving me all alone in the tent.

"Eeek!" I squeaked. "Take me with you!" By then they were too far away to hear me.

Look for more of
HUMPHREY'S TINY TALES

To Priscilla Burris with
THANKS-THANKS-THANKS
for making Humphrey and his friends
come to life in such a wonderful way!
—B.B.

To Craig, Janelle, Laura, Paul—
so grateful for all
the camping memories we share!
—P.B.

Contents

The Creepy-Crawly Classroom

"**W**hat is the opposite of slow?" Mrs. Brisbane asked our class one Friday afternoon.

Mrs. Brisbane is the teacher in Room 26.

I am the classroom hamster.

I was thinking about the answer when Raise-Your-Hand-Heidi Hopper cried out, "Fast!"

"That's correct, Heidi," Mrs. Brisbane said. "But you forgot to raise your hand again."

Heidi said she was sorry, and Mrs. Brisbane continued.

"What is the opposite of happy?" she asked.

A lot of hands went up.

My paw went up, too, but I
guess Mrs. Brisbane didn't notice.
She called on A.J.

"Sad!" he shouted.

"Correct," Mrs. Brisbane said. "But please Lower-Your-Voice-A.J. Now, what's the opposite of silly?"

"Eeek!" a voice cried out.

It was Gail.

She was almost always giggling. That's why I call her Stop-Giggling-Gail.

But she wasn't giggling now. In fact, she looked SCARED-SCARED-SCARED.

"What's the matter, Gail?" Mrs. Brisbane asked.

Gail jumped out of her chair and pointed at her table. "There's a spider!" she said. "A creepy, crawly spider."

"Ewww!" Mandy said.

Og, the classroom frog, splashed around in his water. "BOING-BOING!" he said.

That's the way green frogs like him talk.

"Og likes spiders," Richie said.

It was true. Og likes bugs a lot.

He even likes them for dinner. Ewww!

Mrs. Brisbane walked over to Gail's desk. "It's just a tiny, little spider," she said. "It won't hurt you."

I scrambled up to the tippy top of my cage to get a better look.

The spider must have been tiny, because I couldn't see it at all.

Mrs. Brisbane put a piece of paper under the spider and carried it across the room.

Then she opened the window and gently let the spider crawl outside.

"Girls are scaredy-cats," I heard A.J. whisper loudly.

"They're afraid of everything," his friend Garth agreed.

I don't think girls are scaredy-cats.

I don't think girls are like cats at all.

I also don't think *I'd* be afraid of a tiny spider.

Mrs. Brisbane closed the window. "Boys and girls, most spiders won't hurt you. In fact, they can be helpful," she explained.

I tried to picture a helpful spider.

With eight legs, a spider could be a lot of help when it came to washing dishes and doing other chores.

Mrs. Brisbane said, "They help get rid of pests. And they're very shy."

"But they're creepy," Gail whispered.

Then Mrs. Brisbane asked, "Back to my question: What's the opposite of silly, Gail?"

"Serious," Gail answered.

You know what? For once, she looked VERY-VERY-VERY serious.

~~~~~~~

At the end of the school day, Mrs. Brisbane told the class that Heidi would be taking me home for the weekend.

I'm lucky. As a classroom hamster, I get to go home with a different student each weekend.

Og the Frog stays in the classroom by himself. He doesn't need to be fed every day like I do.

"Bye, Og!" I
squeaked to
my friend
as Heidi
carefully
picked up
my cage. "See
you on Monday!"

"BOING-BOING!" he
replied.

I think Og wished he could
come, too.

So did I.

The Great Outdoors

"Humphrey, we're going on an adventure," Heidi told me in the car on the way home.

"Yippee! What are we doing?" I asked.

I hoped Heidi could understand me, but I knew that all
she heard was "SQUEAK-SQUEAK-
SQUEAK."

"We're camping outside," she
said. "It's finally warm enough."

Maybe she understood me
after all!

Once we
got to the
house, Heidi
took me to
the backyard.
Heidi's dad
was there. He

was hammering a stake in the ground to hold up a big yellow tent.

"Welcome, Humphrey," Mr. Hopper said.

"Thanks!" I squeaked.

I wanted to lend a helping paw, but it would be very difficult for a small hamster to help put up a large tent.

Heidi set my cage on a table.

It was nice to feel the breeze in my fur. And I smelled all kinds of interesting smells, like pine trees and roses.

After a while, I heard a familiar voice ask, "Is Humphrey here?"

It was Miranda, who is also in Room 26. Her name is Miranda Golden. But because she has golden hair, I call her Golden-Miranda.

"We're having a camping night!" I squeaked.

Speak-Up-Sayeh, who is a quiet

girl, also came into the backyard. "I'm so glad you can be with us, Humphrey," she said in her soft, sweet voice.

Then Gail arrived, too. "Is Humphrey going to sleep in the tent with us?" she asked.

"Yes!" Heidi said.

"Eeek!" I squeaked.

I've gone to all kinds of houses and apartments on my weekend outings, but I have never slept outside before.

However, if my friends were sleeping in the tent, then I would, too.

Soon everyone was having a GREAT-GREAT-GREAT time.

The girls hit a ball back and forth over a net. Heidi's mom and dad cooked burgers on a grill.

When it was time to eat, Miranda and Sayeh came over

to my cage and gave me celery sticks and carrots.

They tasted hamster-iffic!

Then, the girls toasted marsh-mallows over the fire. They looked ooey and gooey. But they didn't look like something a hamster would like!

There was so much going on, I hardly noticed that it was growing dark.

"Look up," Mrs. Hopper said to everyone.

Pet hamsters don't spend a lot of time outdoors. We spend even less time outdoors at night.

So when I looked up, I was amazed to see a sky full of twinkling stars.

We studied stars in school, but I never knew they could be so bright.

Mrs. Hopper pointed out that some stars were grouped together and made little pictures.

It was unsqueakably hard to see the pictures at first.

"I see the Big Dipper!" Miranda shouted, pointing at the sky. "See the long handle with a scoop at the end?"

"I see it, too," Gail said.

I stared and stared and then I saw it, too!

"That bright star is the North Star," Sayeh said.

"And Mars is the red-looking planet," Heidi's mom said.

I'd heard a story about green men from Mars invading Earth, so I was a little worried. But when I saw it twinkling, it looked like a very friendly planet.

Then Heidi's dad said, "Let's go for a hike."

"Where will we go?" Heidi asked.

Mr. Hopper smiled and handed each girl a flashlight. "Oh, it will be a *long* hike—all around the yard," he said.

Miranda put me in my hamster ball and set it on the ground.

"Let's look for night crawlers," Mr. Hopper said.

"What are they?" Heidi asked.

"Worms!" Mr. Hopper replied.

"Ewww!" Gail said.

"They sound creepy and crawly," Miranda said.

"Worms won't hurt you," Mr. Hopper explained. "They help the soil."

I crossed my toes and HOPED-HOPED-HOPED he was right.

He led the girls to the back of the yard. I rolled through the grass next to them.

Mr. Hopper handed the girls long sticks. "You might have to dig around a little to find them."

Gail giggled nervously.

I was feeling a little nervous, too.

Then Heidi shouted, "I found some!"

All of us rushed over to the flower bed, where she was poking the earth with her stick.

I was the last to arrive, because it's not easy to roll a hamster ball on the grass.

When Heidi shined her flash-light on the dirt, Sayeh said, "Ooooh!"

"They're creepy," Miranda said.

"And crawly," Heidi added.

Just then, my ball rolled up to the edge of the flower bed.

I agreed. The worms did look crawly and a little creepy. They were slimy and slithery, too.

But they *weren't* scary.

"Creepy-crawlies don't scare me!" I squeaked, which made Gail giggle.

As my friends were busy shining their flashlights around the edge of the yard, my ball hit a little rock and made a sharp turn.

I started rolling away from my friends. I wanted to stop, but the ball kept on rolling.

I ROLLED-ROLLED-ROLLED past the tent and toward the house.

Ahead of me, I saw something very long and very skinny. It reminded me of a worm, but it was much bigger. It was also bright green and it curved all around, just like a snake.

"Eeek!" I shouted.

There was no doubt about it.

I was headed straight toward a great, big green snake!

Boys and Noise

I ran and ran inside my hamster ball, trying to steer it away from the snake.

Suddenly, I was blinded by a bright light.

"There you are, Humphrey!"

Miranda shouted. She scooped up my hamster ball and held it in her hand.

"THANKS-THANKS-THANKS!" I squeaked. "You saved my life."

"Don't be afraid," Miranda said. "That's just the hose. It can't hurt you."

Whew! So the fur-raising snake was really just a harmless hose. But I had to admit that creepy, crawly creatures were a little bit scary after all!

The girls decided it was time to go inside the tent.

There were four sleeping bags on the ground. My cage was on a small wooden table, and Miranda set me inside.

It was dark outside, but it was light inside. There was a tall electric lantern on the table, and the girls had their flashlights.

Heidi taught her friends a funny thing called Morse code.

She had cards with dots and dashes on them. The dots and dashes could be used to spell out words.

The girls could use their
flashlights to send each other
messages on the tent ceiling.

They flicked them on and off to make long and short flashes.

The short flashes were dots. The long ones were dashes.

I didn't have a card, but after Sayeh flicked her flashlight a few times, Miranda said, "You spelled *hello!*"

Heidi spelled a longer word.

"*Camping!*" Sayeh said.

Miranda spelled a really l-o-n-g word.

Gail shouted out, "*Humphrey!*" and everyone laughed.

I'd never seen my name in Morse code before!

Next, Heidi switched on a little box that played music. Soon the girls were all dancing and acting silly.

I did a little dancing myself. Dancing made me forget all about creepy, crawly creatures.

The music was LOUD-LOUD-LOUD.

But suddenly, I couldn't hear the music anymore. I heard a noise that was even louder.

It was a whooping, howling, laughing kind of noise. It was coming from outside the tent.

"What's going on?" Heidi asked. She turned down the music.

"I think it's coming from Richie's yard," Gail said.

Richie was also in Room 26, and he lived next door to Heidi.

The girls peeked out through the tent flap.

"Art and Seth are there with Richie," Miranda said. "And they have a tent set up in the backyard, too."

The noise was VERY-VERY-VERY loud. The boys shouted and shrieked and ran around waving their arms.

Heidi turned up the music. As the music inside the tent got louder, the boys got louder, too.

"That's it," Heidi said, turning

off the music. "I'm going to tell them to be quiet."

Miranda and Gail took their flashlights and went outside with Heidi.

Sayeh took me out of my cage and gently held me in her hands. "You come, too, Humphrey," she said.

When we got near the fence, Heidi shouted, "Could you *please* keep it down? We're having a party over here."

"And we're having a party over here," Richie shouted back.

Then Art noticed me. "Hi, Humphrey," he said. "Why don't you come over here?"

"Yes," Seth said. "You're a boy, too. You belong here."

It's true, I am a boy.

But Mrs. Brisbane sent me home with Heidi for the weekend. It was my job to stay with Heidi.

Art and Seth started making whooping and howling noises again.

"Aren't you girls afraid of the dark?" Richie asked.

"I know they're afraid of spiders," Art said.

"We are not!" Heidi answered.

Then the boys started talking about the bad things that might be outside at night.

Art made a scary face. "Creepy things, crawly things," he said.

"Howling things, growling things," Seth said.

"Ghost and goblin things," Richie said. "*Ooooo.*"

Miranda folded her arms and walked up to the fence.

"Girls aren't afraid of *anything*,"

she said.

"Boys aren't afraid of anything, either!"

Seth said.

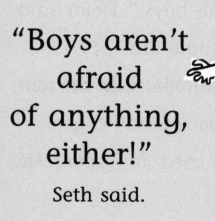

"Ha!" Gail, Heidi, and Sayeh huffed.

"Really?" I squeaked.

Hamsters aren't afraid of many things, except large, furry creatures with huge teeth, like dogs and cats.

I'm not sure about the other scary things the boys described.

"Forget the boys," Heidi said. "Let's have some fun."

Once we were back in the tent, Sayeh put me into my cage.

The girls tried to ignore the

noisy boys. They sat around the lantern and made bracelets out of colorful pieces of string.

"We should make a friendship bracelet for Humphrey," Heidi said.

"It would have to be a tiny one," Gail said.

"But he *is* our friend," Sayeh said in her soft voice.

"YES-YES-YES!" I squeaked, which made Gail giggle.

"Of course!" Gail said.

Sayeh tied a friendship bracelet

to my cage,
which was
unsqueakably
nice.

After a
while, the
boys stopped making noise.

It was nice and quiet. Maybe
it was a little *too* quiet.

"I guess the boys got tired,"
Heidi said.

"Maybe *they're* afraid of the
dark," Gail said.

I heard some shuffling and
whispering kinds of sounds.

"Something's out there," Sayeh whispered.

"It sounds like it's near the tent," Miranda said. "Let's see."

The girls quietly picked up their flashlights and tiptoed to the tent flap.

"There's something in the grass," Gail whispered.

"It's a . . . great . . . big . . . snake!" Heidi shouted.

"Eeek!" the girls screamed.

They raced toward the house, leaving me all alone in the tent.

"Eeek!" I squeaked. "Take me

with you!" By then they were too far away to hear me.

So I did what any small hamster would do. I hid in my bedding and tried to be very still.

It wasn't easy, because I was quivering and shivering.

Then I heard laughter.

I don't think snakes laugh, so I poked my head out of the bedding.

"Did you see those girls run away?" I heard a voice say.

It was Seth talking.

The other boys laughed.

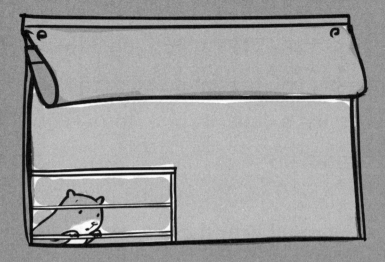

I climbed to the top of my cage so I could see through the tent flap.

There *was* a snake outside. It was VERY-VERY-VERY long. It had a big pointed tongue sticking out of its mouth. It was also very bright green.

And it wasn't moving at all.

I could hear the boys laughing wildly.

"I didn't think girls could run so fast," Richie hooted.

"Or scream so loudly," Seth said.

Art howled with laughter. "And at a rubber snake! I thought girls weren't afraid of *anything*!"

Aha! So the snake wasn't real. It was a fake snake the boys had placed near the tent.

"That's not nice!" I squeaked. But the boys were making too much noise to hear me.

I was upset that the boys had tried to scare the girls.

But I was HAPPY-HAPPY-HAPPY that the long green snake wasn't real!

Out of the Shadows

Then it was quiet again.

I knew there wasn't a real snake in the yard, but I didn't like being alone in the tent.

What if the girls forgot about me? What if they never came back?

I heard someone walking through the grass.

A light was moving around the yard.

I was about to dive under my bedding again when I heard Heidi's dad chuckle.

"So that's the problem!" he said.

I climbed up to the top of my cage and looked out through the tent flap.

Mr. Hopper was holding the toy snake in his hand.

"Girls!" he shouted. "It's safe to come outside again."

A minute later, Heidi and her friends appeared.

"Here's your scary snake," Mr. Hopper told them. "It's made of rubber."

"Those boys are awful," Miranda said.

Heidi agreed. "That was mean."

"It wouldn't be a good camping night without a good scare," Heidi's dad said. "You'll be safe now."

The girls returned to the tent and sat around the table again.

"I'm sorry we ran off without you," Sayeh told me. "We were so scared."

"Let's think of a way to get back at the boys," Heidi said.

"We could throw the snake back in Richie's garden," Miranda suggested.

"That wouldn't fool them," Gail said. "It has to be something really scary."

The girls were quiet again as they tried to think of a plan.

I tried to think of a Plan, too,

but I didn't really like thinking about scary things.

After a while, Heidi turned on the music again. "Let's not let the boys ruin our fun," she said.

Soon, the girls were dancing to the music and laughing.

Then, Heidi's mom came out to the tent. "Time to get into your pajamas and brush your teeth," she said.

Heidi grabbed the big lantern as the girls followed Mrs. Hopper back to the house.

After they left, it was quiet in the tent.

It was lonely in the tent.

It was unsqueakably dark in the tent!

Once in a while, I heard the boys laughing and whispering from Richie's yard.

"Girls!" I heard Seth say.

"Let's take the . . ." Then Art said something I couldn't understand.

All the boys laughed.

Richie said, "That will scare them!"

It sounded as if the boys were planning to scare the girls again. But since the girls weren't around, they'd only end up scaring *me*.

As I sat there in the dark, I noticed that Gail's flashlight was still on the table.

I thought about the lock-that-doesn't-lock on my cage.

Humans always think it's tightly locked, but I have a secret way to open it.

I knew it would be dangerous to be outside my cage, especially in the backyard. But if I could just switch on Gail's flashlight, the tent would be bright and not so scary.

I jiggled the lock and the door opened. I headed straight for the flashlight. It wasn't very far away.

Getting to the flashlight was easy. Turning it on wasn't easy at all.

There was a button on the side, which I pushed and pulled.

The light didn't come on, so I jiggled it and joggled it.

I heard a little *click*.

Suddenly, light shined on one side of the tent. I felt much better.

As I walked back to my cage, I passed in front of the big circle of light. The light was BRIGHT-BRIGHT-BRIGHT, so I turned my head toward the side of the tent.

To my surprise, I saw a very large, very shaggy, VERY-VERY-VERY scary thing.

60

"Eeek!" I squeaked.

I raced toward my cage.

The scary thing raced across the side of the tent.

I turned and ran in the opposite direction.

The scary thing turned and ran in the opposite direction.

I stopped and sat still.

The scary thing stopped and sat still.

THUMPITY-THUMPITY-
THUMP!

My heart was pounding until
I realized that the scary thing
was my very own shadow!

I could hardly believe my eyes.
Who would think that a small
hamster like me could look so
large and scary?

I heard the boys scuffling
outside the tent.

"Shh!" Art said.

"Shh-shh!" Richie said.

I knew they were planning
something creepy and crawly.

But maybe I could scare them first!

I stood in front of the flashlight and got up on my tippy toes. Then I lifted my paw in the air and opened my mouth wide.

I was happy to see that my shadow didn't look like a hamster at all. It looked like a huge and horrible monster.

I looked like a huge and horrible monster.

It was fun to look big for a change.

I opened my mouth even wider

and roared. Of course, all that came out was "SQUEAK-SQUEAK-SQUEAK."

It was quiet outside.

I figured the boys hadn't seen my shadow yet.

I needed to get their attention, so I looked around.

Near me was the little box that made music. I turned it on and music blared.

I reached way up and pawed the air like a scary monster.

And I crossed my toes and hoped that my Plan would work.

The Trouble with Monsters

"It's . . . a . . . monster!" Richie shouted.

"Run for your life!" Art screamed.

"Help!" Seth shrieked.

They howled and yelled. They shouted and screeched.

No matter how loud I screamed, I could never sound as loud as those boys.

As I pawed the air and tried to look big, I heard footsteps running away from the tent.

"Help! Help!" The shrieks moved toward Richie's house.

The yard was quiet again.

I relaxed and stopped acting like a monster.

So, boys were afraid of some things, too!

I hoped the boys weren't *too*

scared, but I was glad that my Plan had worked.

Then I heard footsteps coming toward my tent.

"Eeek!" I squeaked.

I knew it was probably just Mr. Hopper, but I didn't want to be caught outside of my cage. My friends might find out about my secret lock-that-doesn't-lock! And if they did, they might decide to fix it.

Then I'd be stuck in my cage forever and ever!

So I dashed to my cage and pulled the door closed.

"What's going on out here?" Mr. Hopper asked. He poked his head in the tent flap and looked around.

The flashlight was still on and so was the music.

My shadow was on the wall, but now it was my shadow inside the cage.

Mr. Hopper laughed when he saw it. "I think I see what happened," he said.

He left and came back again with Heidi, Gail, Sayeh, and Miranda.

"Are you sure it's safe out here?" Heidi asked. "I could hear those boys screaming from inside the house."

Gail nodded. "I saw them running across the yard."

"I'll show you what scared them," Mr. Hopper said. "Humphrey cast a shadow on the wall of the tent."

He took them around the outside of the tent.

"It looks huge!" Miranda said.

"It looks like a lion in a cage," Sayeh whispered.

"But it wouldn't scare me," Heidi said.

"Me either," Gail agreed. "Silly boys!"

The girls came back into the tent.

"I'm not afraid to be out here," Heidi said.

"Girls aren't afraid of any-thing," Miranda added.

"Girls aren't afraid of anything!" the girls all repeated.

"It's funny, but I don't remember leaving the flashlight on," Heidi said. "Or the music."

Sayeh, Gail, and Miranda didn't remember, either. I didn't squeak up and tell them I had turned them on.

The girls stood between the flashlight and the side of the tent and made funny shadows, like pictures on the wall.

Gail made a crocodile using her hands.

I was just a little bit afraid when she snapped the crocodile's jaws.

Miranda made a bunny rabbit with her hands. It had tall, floppy ears.

Heidi made a dog. She wiggled her fingers and his ears flopped.

75

Then his mouth opened and shut.

"Woof-woof," she barked. That made Gail giggle.

Miranda looked at me. "It's your turn now, Humphrey."

I got up on my tippy toes and raised my paws in the air, like a monster.

The girls saw my shadow and laughed and laughed.

I guess girls aren't afraid of anything after all.

~~~

When it was time for the girls to go to sleep, Heidi's parents came out to the tent.

Mrs. Hopper tucked the girls into their sleeping bags.

I settled down in my bedding.

"Now, get some sleep, girls," Mrs. Hopper said as she left the tent. "You too, Humphrey."

Once we were alone, the tent was QUIET-QUIET-QUIET.

Outside the tent, things weren't so quiet.

First we heard something say, "Whoo-whoooo."

Gail sat up. "What's that?" she asked.

"An owl," Miranda answered. "At least I hope it's just an owl."

Then we heard a fluttering sound, like wings.

"What's that?" Heidi asked.

Miranda sat up and looked around. "It's the tent flap," she said. "At least I hope it's the tent flap."

It was quiet again—almost too quiet.

I was feeling a bit nervous, so I hopped onto my wheel. Spinning always relaxes me.

I forgot that my wheel makes a loud whirring sound. I don't notice it in the classroom, where there are other noises. But in the tent, it sounded unsqueakably loud.

"What's *that*?" Gail asked in a frightened voice.

"I don't know." Miranda sounded even more frightened than Gail.

"It's just me," I squeaked.

"Listen to Humphrey," Sayeh said. "He must have seen something."

Heidi crawled out of her sleeping bag and stood up. "That's it," she said. "I'm sleeping in the house."

"Me too," Gail said.

"Me too," Miranda said.

"And me," Sayeh softly added.

"ME-ME-ME too," I squeaked.

The girls quickly rolled up their sleeping bags. They took their flashlights, the lantern, and my cage back into the house.

As Sayeh carried my cage across the yard, I could see that the tent in Richie's garden was dark.

I was pretty sure the boys had also gone inside.

And even though I didn't see

any *real* creepy, crawly creatures in the garden (besides the night crawlers), I was happy to sleep inside, too.

~~~~~

Heidi took me back to school on Monday morning. When Mrs. Brisbane saw us, she asked how the weekend had been.

"Great," Heidi answered. "I had a camping night in the backyard with my friends."

"So did I," Richie said.

"Oh," Mrs. Brisbane replied. "Were you scared to sleep outside?"

"No," Heidi said. "Girls aren't afraid of anything."

"Neither are boys," Richie added.

They weren't exactly squeaking the truth, but I'm pretty sure they believed what they said.

During class, Mrs. Brisbane asked, "What's the opposite of frightened?"

Richie raised his hand and answered, "Fearless."

~~~~~~

Later that night, I showed Og the friendship bracelet on my cage. Then I told him all about our creepy-crawly camping adventure.

He splashed in his tank and said, "BOING-BOING-BOING-BOING!"

"The girls were scared and the boys were scared," I told my froggy friend. "I wasn't afraid," I said. "At least not much."

But I think that it's all right for girls and boys and even hamsters to be a *little* bit afraid of creepy, crawly creatures.

Even when the scariest thing in the yard turned out to be me!

Look for the next
Humphrey chapter book

Humphrey's
School Fair Surprise